SCRAPING THE

BONE

William Malmborg

DARKER DREAMS
MEDIA

Darker Dreams Media
Chicago, IL

Publisher's Note: This is a work of fiction. Names, characters, places, and incidents are a product of the author's imagination. Locales and public names are sometimes used for atmospheric purposes. Any resemblance to actual people, living or dead, or to businesses, companies, events, institutions, or locales is completely coincidental.

Acknowledgement

The following stories previously appeared in the following publications:

"Red Pickup" in Black Petals, summer 2003
"Jacob's Gift" in Black Petals, fall 2004
"The Bone Yard" in Black Petals, summer 2006
"Code Blue" in the Love & Sacrifice anthology by Zen Films, winter 2007
"Redstone Lake" in Ghostlight, fall 2009

Scraping the Bone / William Malmborg. -- 1st ed.
ISBN:978-0692369968

Contents

Introduction

In 2005, at the age of twenty-one, I came face to face with
a horror that I never imagined possible, one that involved
my own immune system and its inability to tell the
difference between good and bad bacteria. Focusing on
my bowels, specifically the lower end of the small
intestine, my immune system decided to wage war on the
bacteria colonies living within, a *Kill them all, let God sort
them out!*-like motto echoing as it went on the offensive.
The result, severe pain in my lower back and groin
became a daily reality, one that my doctors couldn't
figure out, followed two months later by the sudden onset
of brown, gritty urine that brought tears to my eyes
anytime I needed to use the bathroom. And then one day
I peed out a piece of shredded lettuce.

Shredded lettuce? How is this even possible?

Well, let me tell you.

While attacking the endless supply of bacteria in my small intestine, my immune system couldn't help but also destroy the layers of intestine that the bacteria lived in, damage that it then tried to fix. Over time, the repeated damage and fixings led to two of my organs becoming fuzzed together, one being my small bowel, the other, my bladder. Following that, things that were supposed to go out the backdoor rerouted themselves through a little hole so that they could go out the front.

Imagine living in fear of having to pee, and now imagine having to endure that for nearly a year.

Why a year?

By the time my first doctors figured out what was wrong, my body was too weak for surgery, so they pumped me full of antibiotics to keep the bladder infections from spreading to my kidneys, while also trying to weaken my immune system so that it would stop attacking the bacteria in my bowels. Balancing the two was not easy, and to this day, I have no idea if it really accomplished what they set out for it to accomplish. All I know is, nearly a year later, I started seeing a new doctor, one who took a look at my insides with various imagining tests and gastrological cameras, and tested my blood, all of which alerted him to the fact that I needed surgery as soon as possible because I was dying. Surgery it was, though, with the doctor's okay, my fiancé and I decided to postpone it by three weeks so that I could go down with her to St. Louis where she was being evaluated by a transplant committee to see if she could be added to the waiting list for a new set of lungs.

Um . . . why are you sharing this with us?

Because, 2005 was my most prolific year as a writer. It was also my most successful one up until 2011 when my novel JIMMY found its way into the number one category in several top 100 horror and suspense lists. The reason for this prolific output: the horror I created within my mind helped take me away from the horror of my life. One after another, stories were produced, the pain, anger and hatred within me leveled upon the world of my characters rather than the world of my friends and family. When these stories were entertaining enough upon a reread, I submitted them to magazines and anthologies; when they weren't entertaining and just seemed bitter, I put them in a drawer, their purpose in keeping me sane having been served. Never before had my writing been so important to my survival, both mentally and physically, and only once since then has a similar situation arose, that being while writing a novel titled TEXT MESSAGE.

As both a reader and a writer, fiction, has, to my mind, has one purpose, and that purpose is to momentarily release the one that sits down with it from their daily existence, and thrust them into a situation that, while possibility familiar, is still different enough to provide intrigue and a desire to know what will happen next. With horror fiction, there is an added element of generating a fear response, one that is being administered safely since those involved know they will be coming out of the experience unscathed.

The stories that follow in this collection are ones that I believe provide that momentary release, as well as a fear response for those that crave such things. Two were written prior to the events of 2005, two after, six during. Half of them were published in magazines and anthologies, the other half were accepted, but never saw publication due to the publications they were supposed to appear within folding.

Redstone Lake

No! Oh god! No! Dark water flooded his mouth. It had that unnatural fishy taste of lake water. It wasn't salty, but definitely not pure, and most certainly undrinkable.

Arms flailing, he tried to get back to the surface, but the hold was too strong. Slowly but surely the water filled his screaming lungs. Then, nothing but darkness.

* * *

Tim. Honey. Tim. "It's okay. Wake up."

Tim opened his eyes and looked at his wife Kim who was standing before him, her hands on his shoulders. She was wearing the red robe he had gotten her for Christmas; only it was unbelted and did little to cover her nakedness.

Nakedness? He remembered the two of them making love the night before. At first it had started with a few gentle kisses, but then had gotten hotter and hotter until they had ended up in bed tearing at each others clothing.

"You okay?" she asked.

"Um . . ." confusion racked his brain. He looked around. *What had happened?* Despite the peaceful surroundings he felt terrified. *Something awful had happened.* "I'm fine."

"Nightmare?" she asked.

He rubbed at his eyes. Brittle crusts fell away. He remembered the lake and the girl. Something grabbing him. "Yeah. A nightmare."

"Must've been a bad one. Come on, let's get some breakfast before we leave." She started walking out of the room.

"Leave?" he asked.

Kim stopped and looked at him. "Ha, ha, come on."

* * *

Tim's great grandfather had built the old log cabin before the turn of the century back when the country was still young. The man had been born during the Civil War and lived to the end of the Second World War. Since then the cabin had gone through serious renovations while being handed down from father to son, father to son, until it reached Tim.

"I can't believe you never told me about this place," Kim said while stepping out of the car. It had been a seven-hour drive from Chicago to the north woods of Wisconsin. Both were eager to walk around, yet Tim did not get out of the car right away.

He had forgotten about the place for several years, just recently being reminded of it when his wife found a picture in the back of his desk drawer. *What had she been doing in his desk?* This had been a couple of months ago. Almost instantly she had confronted him about the place and demanded they go visit it sometime. Now they were here.

A sense of dread engulfed him.

"You coming?" Kim asked.

Tim didn't respond.

Turn around, his mind pleaded. *Leave. Go home. Now!*

These strange thoughts had been appearing throughout the drive north from the moment the car had left the garage, yet he had no idea why.

"Tim? TIM!"

He jerked his head to Kim's door, which was open. Kim stood by it, crouching down and peering in. "Uh . . . what?" he asked.

"What's wrong?" she asked.

He shook his head. "Nothing. I'm fine." He pulled the keys out of the ignition – *who would steal the car way out here, there's no one around for miles* – and stepped out. *No one around for miles.* The thought sent a chill down his spine. "Let's go inside and look around a bit before getting the bags."

Tim hoped to God something would be wrong inside that would force them to leave -- rotten floorboards, broken pipes, animals, crumbling foundation -- anything. With the bags still on the car all they would have to do was walk out and drive away.

The cabin was in great shape.

* * *

Redstone Lake was so named due to a red rock formation in the middle of the water. Nothing grew on the rocks and they were only large enough for a few people to walk on. However, they were surprisingly soft and it was not uncommon to see

....

someone lying down upon them after rowing a boat
out, usually with a simple towel protecting their back.

"That's why it's called Redstone?" Kim asked after
they had gotten settled in. Together they sat on the
screened porch watching the lake.

"Yeah. There's red rocks beneath the surface as
well, dotted all over the lake. That's why no one has
any motor boats or jet skies." Which in turn was one
of the reasons why the lake wasn't that popular.

"I like it like this. It seems more -- I don't know --
natural." Kim shrugged. "How are the stars at
night?"

This comment made Tim uneasy again.

"Tim?" Kim asked. "Tim."

He jerked his head to her. "What?"

"I asked you a question. What's wrong with you?
Ever since we got here you've been acting strange."
She was getting that motherly tone he did not like. All
girls seemed to have it.

"It . . . I don't know. It's been so long. Too many childhood memories." Actually, there were no childhood memories that he could think of. Tim had no idea what was making him uneasy. It had something to do with the water, and his dream the night before. *Did I almost drown?*

No. If that were the case, he would have trouble with the pool as well, which he didn't. And when at the ocean he could swim for hours without a problem.

"What childhood memories?"

"I don't know. Just forget it, all right? I don't know why I'm uneasy." He looked out at the water. As the sun lowered in the sky it reflected off the calm lake surface. Slowly the shadows grew. Darkness was coming.

* * *

Tim, I'm waiting. The words were coming from the rocks in the middle of the lake. Tim stood on the rickety pier, listening. At the moment he had no fear, just curiosity. Who was out there?

* * *

"No. Kim. I'm not going. Please. I don't want to go out there." Only, a part of him, remembering the dream from the night before, did.

"Why not?" Kim demanded. "I spent all morning getting the boat into the water and now you don't want to go." Her anger was not hidden. The hard work of getting the boat into the water from the small shed was obvious. Sweat covered her body and plastered her hair against her forehead.

"No one told you to put the boat in the water." Tim hated it when people – Kim – simply assumed he wanted to do something.

"For God sake, we're on a lake." She crossed her arms, a sign that she was really pissed. "Why did you come up here?"

"I don't know," he shouted back. "Maybe that was a mistake." He started walking back up to the cabin, then stopped and came back down. "Fine. Let's go row the boat."

"Not if you're gonna be all ticked off," Kim said.

"No. You wanted to go for a boat ride. Well, I'm here. *Let's go.*"

Now she turned and headed up for the cabin.

What the hell? Tim asked himself. *Why do girls do that?* They wanted one thing one second, then something else the next. It was so irritating. *Damn.* He picked up a small stone and threw it against the trunk of a tree.

* * *

They started speaking again around dinner that night, after going into town and eating burgers at the Village Tavern. The place reeked of smoke and noise, but was a good distraction from the solitude they had both been suffering at the lake.

"Do you want to go back home?" Kim asked as they were eating. "Obviously this place is affecting you."

Tim thought honestly about this for several seconds

and then shook his head. "We can stay. I just . . . I'm sorry for getting upset this morning." He sipped his beer, his mouth savoring the aftertaste of the cool liquid as it slipped down his throat.

"What happened?" she asked.

"I don't know?" He couldn't tell her that he had a strange and sudden fear of the lake, could he? Or that he wanted to be as far away from the cabin as possible?

His mind drifted back to the nightmare he had the other day. Obviously Chicago had not been far enough.

"Be honest. Why didn't you tell me about the cabin? Did something happen to you when you were a kid?"

"No. What makes you think that?" Tim asked with a small laugh. His response was a little too quick.

"Earlier you said 'too many childhood memories' remember?" What memories were you talking about?"

Tim didn't know.

* * *

That night Tim once again heard his name being called and went from his warm comfortable bed to the cool rickety pier. The shiver that passed through him was not due to the cold, but the sound of the voice echoing over the water. This time, however, it was not a dream. He was out there for real, which meant the calling of his name was for real as well.

"Tim?"

He shouted and spun around. Kim was standing there, her robe tight around her body.

"What are you doing out here? *Oh my Lord*, look at the stars."

Tim followed her gaze up into the heavens. This far north there was hardly any blackness between the small dots of light and one could really appreciate the name *Milky Way*.

"Tim, I'm waiting." These words were coming from the rocks again. Tim looked over at Kim who was still looking up at the stars. Obviously she had not heard the voice. Had she, then the stars would be the furthest thing from her mind.

"You know. I've always wondered what it would be like to make love underneath the stars," Kim said.

Tim looked at her. "What?"

She stepped closer, her robe falling open. A gentle breeze played with her hair. Then, before he knew it, she was pulling him down upon the pier, her hands opening his robe and exploring. Tim couldn't resist.

* * *

Tim opened his eyes. Above him the stars swayed back and forth. His back was damp. All around him he heard the gentle caress of water as it pushed itself against surrounding surfaces. In the trees an owl called out.

And then suddenly there was the sound of scraping

metal, and the rocking of the stars above turned to a terrible jolt.

Tim sat up, which caused further rocking. For a moment he had no idea what he was looking at, but then realized it was the lake. He was surrounded by dark water, the shoreline barely visible off in the distance.

There was that scraping sound again. Tim jerked his head to the right. The dark surface of the water was broken by the smooth surface of rock, which the boat had bumped up against.

Why am I in the boat?

This sparked a strange fear within him.

"You came back."

"Ahhh!" Tim screamed. The voice was right next to him yet the source still unseen.

"I always knew you would."

The boat suddenly tipped, spilling Tim into the cold

dark water. His scream was cut off midway by water flooding his mouth. He couldn't help but swallow the unclean substance and then began choking as his head broke the surface.

Overturned, the boat quickly drifted away.

Something grabbed his foot.

Tim screamed again and kicked. His foot was free, but whatever had grabbed him was trying to get it back. He had to get out of the water.

The rocks.

He splashed his way forward, his legs kicking furiously behind him. It took only a second to reach the rocks and crawl up on them.

His wet robe clung to his cold body. He wrapped his arms around himself trying to hold in heat. It didn't work and within seconds he was shivering uncontrollably.

And then he saw something in the water. At first he thought it was the reflection of stars above him, but then slowly realized it was a face. A girl. She was looking at him.

He shouted.

The face drew nearer. A voice came out of the water from it. *"I always knew you'd come back for me. True love knows no boundaries."*

"NO!" Tim screamed while moving backward. Unfortunately there wasn't much space and he only managed a few inches. "GO AWAY!"

"Tim!" a voice called over the water. It was Kim.

"KIM! HELP ME!"

The face drew nearer and nearer. Tim remembered the last time he had seen that face. It had been drifting away from him, Jenny's blood still on his hands from where her head had struck the rocks after their struggle.

It's too late, he had said earlier that day.

No. I changed my mind. Please. I can't do this, Jenny

had said back while trying to stand, one hand grabbing her swimsuit while the other tried to cover her nakedness, her body bumping up against his several times as the two tried to balance on the wet rocks.

Tim lost his balance and reached for her, his hand yanking her arm hard as he tried to hold his footing.

Jenny yanked back as she started to fall forward but over did it and shouted as her feet went right out from under her.

A terrible *thunk* echoed as her head bounced against the rock. All struggle stopped. Tim, horrified, bent forward, his manhood hanging forgotten, and looked at her head. Blood oozed backward into the water.

"Together forever," Jenny now said, jerking Tim's mind back to the present. *"Isn't that what we once wrote?"* Her face broke the surface and appeared before him.

Tim saw himself pushing her body into the water

all those years ago, not before putting her swimsuit

back on, however. Luckily she hadn't brought him far

enough along for there to be any of his fluids in or on

her.

"Go away!" he shouted. "It was an accident. Go

away." He kicked at her but she just grabbed his leg.

There was strength in that grip – strength unlike he

had ever felt before.

A quick tug pulled him into the water, his back

easily gliding against the smooth rock. The hand

continued to pull against him and soon he was

beneath the surface, arms struggling against the water

without success.

He tried holding his breath, his mouth shut tightly

against the water that wanted in.

"You didn't even try to help me, did you? All you cared

about was making sure no one blamed you."

Tim couldn't hold it anymore and took a deep

breath. Cold, dark water flooded his mouth and went

down his throat. It tasted awful, yet he couldn't help

himself and gulped more and more until it filled his
lungs.

"Together forever," Jenny said as his life left him.

* * *

"I don't know," Kim insisted the next morning to the
town sheriff. "He seemed happy until we got here
and then something wasn't right." She fought back
tears. "Did you find him?" The sheriff had been out
on the water for a long time, over by the red rocks
with one of his deputies.

Earlier that morning Kim had woken alone on the
pier, Tim's shout across the water waking her. She
hadn't been able to see him but felt that his location
was somewhere near the red rocks, where she later
directed the sheriff.

"Yes, ma'am, we found him. I'm sorry." He had
never seen anything like it before. Her husband had
tied two large cinder blocks to his ankles before
tipping over his boat near the red rocks. The water in
that area was only ten feet deep. Had the rope been a

foot longer the man's face would have broken the surface and he would have survived. "I'll need you to come down to the station and answer a few questions."

Rest Stop

I'm watching you.

Carol read the message carved into the bathroom door and shivered. Had she not already committed her flesh to the grimy toilet seat she would have gotten up and changed stalls. One dose of mysterious bacteria was enough, however, no matter how unpleasant the décor.

Relief came quickly. For an hour she had been clutching her thighs together, the courage-inducing liquor she had downed earlier wanting an escape. Carol had refused to pull over. Not until she was far enough away from the bastard to feel safe. Had her bladder not been about to burst she would have put more miles between them and Terry, but alas nature had won the battle.

Kelly was asleep in the car. Carol had been unwilling to wake the five year old. A good shake would have been enough, but she couldn't do it. Waking her up once, telling her to be quiet, and then driving her away from her father without an explanation had been enough trauma for one night. Questions would come eventually, but that moment hadn't arrived. In time her daughter would realize this was all for the best.

The door to the bathroom opened.

Footsteps echoed.

"Kelly?" Carol called even though the steps seemed awfully heavy for a child. A terrible thought entered. *What would Kelly think if she woke up in an empty car in the middle of nowhere?*

They were most certainly in the middle of nowhere. Carol had gotten on the expressway after leaving Terry and just headed South at about eighty miles an hour. The lack of traffic would have allowed her to go faster, but she had managed some control. The last town, Haddonfield, had been ten miles back.

Since then nothing but trees and some old abandoned houses had lined the road.

"Hello?" Carol asked as the footsteps continued.

Silence.

A chill danced across her spine.

Not only were the footsteps too heavy to be that of a child, but they seemed too heavy to be a woman.

Carol wanted to say something else but couldn't bring herself to do it. Instead she bent forward and looked under the stall door. A pair of long trench boots stood a few inches away. She couldn't see the rest of him.

He was standing right outside her door.

Fear hit.

Carol didn't know what to do. The silence was bad, but speaking was out of the question, even though he had to know she was there. Even her bladder had clamped up.

Her heartbeat quickened.

Eventually the silence got to be too much.

"What do you want?" she asked. She wanted to sound forceful but couldn't manage it. Any courage the liquor had given her earlier was long gone. Exhaustion and fear filled the void.

No answer.

Earlier she had been ready to do whatever was necessary to take Kelly from her abusive husband. The slap hadn't been particularly hard, and most certainly wasn't the worst thing he had ever done to her, but had been the last straw. Terry had passed out after that. His evening ritual of drinking a twelve pack of tall boys once dinner was complete always knocked him out. Carol would have said something about his drinking years ago, but knew it often led to long nights of silence, which she cherished. He was only mean during the first few beers. After that, it was somewhat pleasant.

The man outside the stall didn't say anything or do

anything. Carol peeked under the door again. He was still there.

What did he want?

Open the door and do something, Carol's mind urged. One good kick from him would rip the door from its frame so opening it wouldn't exactly be dumb. At the same time, she didn't want to make the situation any easier. She wasn't like that anymore. She wasn't the woman who would stand still while Terry beat her so as not to make him any angrier by running or fighting back. Her hands had always tried to protect her face, but that was it.

Carol looked under the door again.

The boots were still there, laces open and dangling onto the stained tile floor. What was the rest of him like? And why was he just standing there?

She pictured a man waiting by a stall door; his hands ready to grab the helpless woman within once the door was open. She was that woman, but was she really helpless?

Her purse was sitting atop the plastic toilet paper dispenser. Inside was a small can of pepper spray. Her husband, a former police officer, had once given it to her in case anything happened while walking to her car. This had been back before he started drinking heavily, and while she had still worked the evening shift at a bar called Strike Three in Chicago. Unfortunately she hadn't been able to get the spray out in time one night six years earlier. Even if she had, the chances of fighting off three young men (she assumed they were young but couldn't tell because of the ski masks) were pretty slim. She probably could have taken one or two out with the pepper spray, but not the third.

She pulled the can of spray from her purse.

The rape had been the start of it all. Terry had never been able to catch the bastards. For over a year he spent all his time around that bar hoping they would come back, but they never did. He also put continuous pressure on the DNA team to find a match, but they never came up with anything.

Carol got the spray ready. Now all she needed was the courage to open the door. One shot in the eyes with the spray and the guy wouldn't be able to do anything to her.

One shot with the spray six years earlier and Kelly might never have been born.

Carol pushed that thought away. Being raped was bad enough, but not being able to wish it away for fear that her wonderful baby girl would never have been born was worse.

"Mommy!" Kelly screamed.

Her daughter's voice mustered the courage she needed. Carol twisted the lock and yanked the door back.

No one was there.

The shoes were empty.

"Mommy!" Kelly screamed again.

Carol raced from the bathroom.

A dark car was skidding out of the gravel parking lot. Kelly was inside, her tiny fists pounding on the back window.

Carol ran.

The car was faster.

Carol went to her own car. Even in the darkness she could see that all four tires were flat. This didn't stop her from getting in and trying to give chase. It was no use, though. By the time, she pulled out of the rest stop the car was nowhere to be seen.

Jacob's Gift

"Oh my God! He's alive. Stop! He's alive. Don't bury him!" Jacob's shouts silenced the small crowd of gatherers who had come to mourn and watch little Timmy being put to rest. Father Jessup stood startled, his small funeral Bible threatening to fall from his arthritic hands.

Jacob looked around at his family's faces. There was pity upon them -- pity for him, he realized. It was so sad. Young Jacob losing his even younger brother and then thinking he was still alive. So sad.

Jacob felt anger arise at their known thoughts and shouted, "He's not dead," and turned back to Timmy's body. The chest which had taken a deep breath just moments before was still again.

Tears began to fall from Jacob's eyes. *No,* he thought. *You can't be dead. Please don't be dead.* The chest suddenly rose again. "HE'S ALIVE!" Jacob shouted.

A hand came out of nowhere and took Jacob's arms and pulled him back. There was fury in the grip, but fury that would be held back until a more appropriate time. His mother would never punish him in front of these people. No. They would not tolerate it, especially not now. "Jacob honey, you're going to have to let go. Timmy needs you to let go." His mother had tears in her eyes, tears that smeared her black mascara. She had only worn it so it would smear and that way make her sadness even more pronounced.

"But he's alive. I saw him breathing."

Mother was embarrassed by his obvious madness and quickly glanced at the gatherers. They all turned their heads away, as if none of this was being seen or acknowledged.

Jacob turned his head back in the direction of

Timmy's casket and thought to himself. *Please get up.*
Show them you're not dead.

There was a sudden gasp from the crowd and for a
moment Jacob thought that Timmy had listened and
risen. He hadn't. But his casket had suddenly tipped
and threatened to fall. Uncle Ben stopped this from
happening completely.

Everyone thought it was a gust of wind or some
earth tremor. Jacob, however, knew the truth. Timmy
had tried to get up but failed. Even people who had
seen his attempt would deny it later, for things like
that didn't happen in the real world. Little boys who
had drowned in pools earlier in the week didn't get up
from their caskets. That just didn't happen.

Jacob received several painful paddle strikes when
he got home later that day and then was locked in his
bedroom without being served dinner. "Don't ever
embarrass me like that again in front of my family,"
were the words that accompanied the punishment.
Nothing was said about Timmy. Mother didn't really
care that he had died.

That night while lying on his stomach (not his back because it was too painful from the paddle) Jacob thought about Timmy and what it was like for him at that moment. Though he had pleaded with his family not to bury him, the casket had been closed, lowered, and sealed into the earth by dirt. Poor Timmy. He would awaken while buried and then suffocate to death. Not before breaking all his fingernails and wearing his fingertips to the bone trying to claw his way out. Poor Timmy. How long would it take? How much air would be trapped within the casket? Would it be like drowning all over again?

* * *

After several minutes of thinking about this Jacob couldn't stand it anymore and rose from his bed. A groan escaped his lips as his back cried out, but it was the only sound he made.

Putting his ear to the door, he listened for his mother. If she were awake, she would be making a sound, unless she was once again listening to see if he really were sleeping.

The punishment he had received earlier would probably have satisfied her for the night and the silence was a true one. Using the paperclip he kept stored under his desk, Jacob opened the locked door. He had learned how to do this several months earlier after the terrible night his mother had given him a laxative with dinner and then locked him in the bedroom. His cries to be let out and use the bathroom had been met with laughter from her.

Since then he had vowed never to be locked in the bedroom again while needing to go to the bathroom and learned how to open the door.

There was a loud *click* and then the door was open. Jacob waited to see if the sound had been heard. The house stayed silent.

Jacob pushed open the door and stepped out into the hallway.

Before his father's death, Jacob had been given a bike for his birthday. He had just begun to learn how to ride it when his father had the heart attack. After that, his mother forbid him to use the bike for reasons unknown, but kept it around so family members could see what a good parent she was. So good, she had given her son a bike for his birthday.

Fortunately, the saying was correct and Jacob had never forgotten how to ride.

Because his mother kept his shoes locked up at night in her closet, Jacob had to ride the bike barefoot. Thankfully it was summer and the night warm, so his toes did not turn into little ice cubes.

The cemetery where Timmy had been laid to rest was a little over three miles from their home and it would have taken only twenty minutes for him to ride if he hadn't had to duck behind something whenever headlights appeared on the horizon. Adults didn't like kids to be out after dark. It was dangerous.

Thirty-five minutes after leaving his house, Jacob arrived at the gate of the cemetery. A broken camera looked at him from a post behind the gate, its lens long ago shattered by a rock.

Jacob first put his bike through the bars of the gate

and then turned himself sideways and slipped in.
There were advantages to being a child, slipping
through things adults couldn't was one of them.

Graveyards were spooky after dark, but rarely
dangerous. His uncle had told him this just that
morning as they made their way along the path
toward the spot where Timmy would be buried. Jacob
had already known this but nodded anyway, at the
same time wondering what his mother would have
done with Timmy if there were no relatives to please.
Certainly she wouldn't have spent money on a grave
plot, casket and stone. Knowing her she probably
would have secretly cut up the body, cooked it, and
then told Jacob it was turkey. Once he finished eating
she would inform him of the truth, just like his pet cat
a few months earlier. She liked doing things like that.
Jacob wasn't sure why and often wished she didn't.

There was a strange presence floating throughout
the graveyard that Jacob had felt earlier in the day but
had been unsure of what to make of it. When he asked
his uncle about it he had said that sometimes the
energy of the dead stays with their body because it

didn't know what to do.

You have to be pretty special to feel it my, boy. Like your father. Jacob wasn't sure what to make of this statement and had wanted to ask his uncle about it, but couldn't because his mother had walked up at that moment and taken his hand. He did know one thing, being special meant you were unlike others, so that meant he was part of a few who could feel this energy.

It seemed to float around him as he walked down the quiet road, his bike rolling next to him.

Timmy's grave was located on a hillside that was sunny during the day and bathed in moonlight at night. Because of this moonlight, Jacob saw from a distance that something wasn't right about the gravesite. As he got closer he realized that the dirt was missing. Someone had dug Timmy up.

For the first time that night a chill ran down his spine and sprang the hairs on his neck erect.

Who would do this? Certainly not Timmy, for the casket below was still closed and solid. He would

have to claw his way through first and then dig. That
hadn't happened.

"I knew you'd return my boy," a familiar voice said
from the darkness.

Jacob whirled around and watched as his uncle
stepped out from behind an oak tree. He was too
shocked to speak.

"I'm guessing your mother does not know you're
here?"

Jacob nodded.

"Very good. She wouldn't like what I have to tell
you."

"You dug him up?" Jacob asked as soon as he
found his voice.

His uncle nodded. "I knew you would call him up,
though I have to admit, even I was startled when his
coffin tipped. I suppose your power was fueled by
your sadness at seeing him."

Jacob shook his head. "What power?"

"You have a gift, Jacob. I've known it ever since your father came and knocked on my door several nights after I witnessed him buried. Unfortunately, his fingers had been worn away from clawing his way out and will never be useful again. Dead cells don't heal themselves."

Once again Jacob could not speak. He remembered dreaming about his father being alive in his coffin, but hadn't done anything to call him up -- or whatever his uncle was talking about. That just couldn't happen.

As if on cue, a figure stepped out from behind the tree and stood next to his uncle. Jacob gasped loudly. Despite the rotting flesh and worn clothing, he still recognized his father. His hands were terribly mangled.

His uncle studied Jacob's father for a second and then said, "At one point he could speak but his tongue and mouth have rotted since then. He told me you called him up and that he needed to serve you. I of course couldn't let him return to you until I understood what was going on myself and got over the shock of seeing my dead brother."

Jacob saw the marks upon his father's wrists and realized he had been bound for a long time. "You tied him up?"

"He wanted to return to you and would have if I hadn't restrained him," he said. "Now, I believe you have someone waiting for you down there."

Jacob shifted his eyes to the closed casket and wanted to believe that his brother was once again alive, only knew that it was impossible -- even after seeing his father here.

His uncle grew impatient and suddenly jumped down and pulled open the casket. Frightened eyes stared up at him and an unearthly cry rose out of Timmy's dead lips.

Jacob was terrified by what he saw and wanted to run away, yet was also fascinated and stood his ground so he could see what would happen next.

Timmy shifted his gaze toward Jacob and suddenly sat up. "Thank you," he said through his cold lips. It sounded false.

His uncle was more excited than Jacob and jumped up and down shouting. *"I knew it, I knew it. Your father did this with our pet dog once, but you can do it with people."*

At the same time Jacob looked into Timmy's mind -- he wasn't sure how -- and saw something terrible. He saw his uncle in the pool holding down Timmy's head until his body stopped jerking about.

"Just think of the things you can do, the army you could create -- "

"You did this to him," Jacob said suddenly, his eyes staring down at his uncle.

"Well . . . what do you mean?" his uncle asked, his voice startled by Jacob's sudden change.

"You drowned him."

"I . . . I knew you'd bring him back up. I had to so

you would -- "

"You killed him to see if I would bring him back to life." Anger was rushing through him and now he decided to see how far his power went.

His uncle was about to say something but his voice was cut off by the sudden grip of two hands upon his throat.

His father's hands, though mangled, could still grip large objects such as a neck.

Hysterical hands reached out and took hold of his father's worn clothing and began pulling. The clothing snapped and the hands fell back. His uncle would have fallen as well but his father's grip was too much.

The struggling went on for another minute, though each second his uncle got weaker and weaker. Finally his body collapsed.

Jacob had watched without emotion as his dead father strangled his uncle to death. At the same time

Timmy had climbed out of the grave and now stood, waiting, his body lifeless except for the fact that he was standing there.

His father let go of his uncle and the three (though Jacob felt that he was really the only one) watched as his body fell to the ground.

A new wave of energy joined the air. Jacob felt it almost calling for him. He could raise his uncle up and use him, or leave him to rot. Actually, either way he would rot, but was the rotting painful once a body was called up, or just like being dead?

Jacob called up his uncle and ordered him to get into the grave Timmy had lain in since this morning and then ordered Timmy to fill the dirt back in.

There was no satisfaction in knowing that his uncle was lying in there till he rotted away. In fact, Jacob wished his father hadn't killed him and only struggled with him until he got him into the coffin and then buried him alive. That would have been better.

Oh well.

Jacob looked from his brother to his father, then at all the silent graves. Could he call all of them up as well? Why not?

His uncle had said something about creating an army. Sure. There were way more dead people than living people on earth. But what condition did they have to be in? What good was someone whose legs had rotted away, or someone who would fall apart at the slightest touch?

There were some things he would have to learn about this power, some experiments he would have to perform. Tonight was not the night for this, however. What he wanted now was to get back home and have his father quietly ease himself between the sheets of his mother's bed and snuggle up against her. Then, later, when she woke, she would be staring at her dead husband. It would be the first of several long, terrible things that would happen to her at the hands of the dead -- the hands of Jacob.

The Phone Call

Tom sat in his favorite leather chair staring at the phone, his mind silently willing it to ring, wanting it to ring, *needing* it to ring.

The phone stayed silent.

Staring at it did not help, yet he could not look away. Hours had gone by. The sun had set. Shadows had grown. Darkness descended. It was time.

Another hour passed.

The phone rang twice as the minutes ticked by, but neither caller was her. First it had been a salesman, a

•••

fact he had known before answering due to the caller ID, the second one a wrong number.

His nerves stood at attention.

The silence was bad, but having the phone ring -- that sudden wonderful sound -- and it not being her was worse. Hearing the ring was like listening to the lottery numbers being drawn and having all of them correct but the last. In the end, due to the build up of excitement, and then the terrible letdown, it would have been better not to have any of the numbers at all.

Ring dammit!

The phone stayed silent, mocking him.

She's not going to call, the mean voice said.

Yes she will, the nice one replied. *She has the number.*

Laura did too.

Laura.

His mind drifted back a few years. At the time he had been working as a dishwasher and Laura was one of the waitresses. She had been beautiful. A real catch. One to have for all time. Yet it hadn't worked.

Tom never was sure what had gone wrong, though he had some theories. In the end, however, those theories didn't matter. He had given her his number, yet she had never called, which meant something had gone wrong. Nothing would change that.

Is the same thing going to happen tonight?

No. She has the number. Everything's fine. It's going to work. She's going to call.

The mean voice did not reply. It didn't need to. The silent phone was aggravating enough.

Tom's eyes drifted over to the wall clock and calculated how many hours had passed. Worry twisted his bowels. If she didn't call soon she probably never would.

Please call. You have the number. You have the phone. What else do you need?

Nothing came to mind. It never did. Once again, if

she failed to call, all he would have was theories on what had gone wrong. Those theories would never be proven. Once they didn't call it was too dangerous to go and find out why.

His eyes went from the clock to the small piece of paper sitting next to the phone. Her number was there, written neatly. He stared at if for a long time, but didn't pick up the phone.

After the last girl, he had started writing down the cell phone numbers just in case everything worked yet they didn't call. He always assumed they would be smart enough to see his number written on the piece of paper and make the call, but perhaps this was just wishful thinking. People weren't always as bright as they sometimes seemed. It was also possible that their intelligence didn't return with them. If that were the case, they probably wouldn't pick up the phone if it rang and spend the rest of their days lying beneath the dirt.

You should dig them up, see if it has worked, the mean voice said. *They're all waiting.*

Tom wondered if this was a lure to get him in trouble, or if the voice really thought they were alive again down there? His mind wanted to lean toward the latter, but feared the former. The mean voice was always getting him in trouble. It enjoyed watching him suffer at the hands of others, and had accomplished this many times in the past.

The dog was a good example. One day while walking home from school, he saw a puppy sitting in a car next to White Hen. Normally he would try his experiments on creatures that were completely isolated and would not be missed. That day, however, the mean voice said it could feel the power and that the dog would be the one. Tom had listened, and nearly gotten caught when the owner of the car came running out demanding to know what he was doing with his puppy.

Tom got away that day, but barely, and in the end it hadn't worked. The dog, like everything else since the fish, had remained lifeless once the last breath was choked from it.

Another hour drifted away.

Tom got up from his chair and stretched his legs. From his window he looked out at the graveyard behind his house. He wondered if he had ever called any up without knowing. What if it only happened in his sleep and that was the reason why he never could bring the animals or people back?

His mind drifted into the past to when he was five years old. He had been sleeping when he brought his fish back to life. Many years had passed since that amazing experience yet he remembered it well. His mother had told him the fish was just sleeping and would probably be better in the morning. Tom, however, knew the truth and spent most of the night wishing the creature back to life. At some point he had drifted off to sleep. When he woke up his wish had come true. The fish was alive, its small golden body darting back and forth around the glass bowl. It was this experience that made him first wonder if he, like Jesus, could bring things back from the dead.

Unfortunately, his power had only worked on the

fish thus far, and only back when he was younger.
Some weeks he had purposely forgotten to feed the
small swimmer until it died, yet the next day it was
always back, the oldest goldfish alive.

Tonight would be different. The realization that he
had been sleeping whenever the fish was brought back
mixed with the reasoning that perhaps they didn't
know how to use the phone made him believe in the
possibility that he had brought everyone back without
knowing it. All this time he had been waiting for a
phone call from the men and women he had taken,
when really what he needed to do was go and dig
them up. They weren't going to call. Knowledge was
lost once a person died. He would have to teach them
everything over again.

Or was that really the case? What if he dug up the
body and someone happened to be walking by.
Terrible things could happen if someone saw him out
there fooling around with the dead. Worse, at some
point someone might find out that he was responsible
for their deaths, which wouldn't be good. People
didn't believe in powers like that anymore, not even

his mother. She had wanted to put him away once she found out about his experiments with the animals and had almost made it to the phone before Tom hit her over the head with the frying pan.

He hadn't meant to hit her so hard, or really to hit her at all. The fear of being locked up in a small white padded room had caused him to act irrationally. Unfortunately, he couldn't take his actions back, but he could right the wrong once he learned how to bring people back from the dead.

Time was running out, though. Talk of pulling the plug on his mother's brain dead body was on the rise. The insurance money was running out and no one in his family could afford to keep the treatments going.

Tom had no idea how long he would have once she died. Furthermore, he wouldn't want to bring her back if her body was rotting away. What kind of life would that be? Could they do plastic surgery on a body that had already died?

This was just one of the many mysteries he could not answer until he finally brought a person back from the dead.

Exhaustion hit.

Tom closed his eyes and tried to fall asleep. In the morning he would go and dig up Nancy's body and see if she was waiting for him. If not, he would try some of the others and see if they were. Until then, he would just rest and let the power work in whatever way it wanted. He was tired anyway. Hunting a person down and strangling them to death was quite the workout, especially when they fought so hard.

The Other Side

1 OFFLINE MESSAGE.

Michael stared at the note as his computer finished booting up, his mind spinning. It had been over a month since Linda had spoken with him online and he had finally decided she no longer liked him. But now there was a message waiting, and he hadn't contacted anyone else since Linda. Could the message be from her?

Linda hadn't been the first person to suddenly stop talking with Michael. In fact, the entire Internet dating scene had been one long string of disappointments. Five times he had made contact with girls that seemed

just right for him, and five times they had talked for
weeks and weeks until the girl eventually broke it off.
They weren't good breaks either. Everything would
be going smoothly when all of the sudden no more
messages would appear. Michael would send out
messages but they would all be deleted or ignored.
One minute he would be excited that he had finally
found someone to be his first girlfriend, the next he
would realize he had been rejected, again.

But maybe there had been a good reason for
Linda's lack of communication? Perhaps she had been
out of town for a month and hadn't been able to
contact him? And now a message was waiting that
would say something like: SORRY I'VE BEEN AWAY.
I MISSED TALKING TO YOU. LET'S MEET
FINALLY AND REALLY GET TO KNOW EACH
OTHER. LINDA.

The two had talked about meeting before she
stopped messaging him, but nothing had
materialized. Now, however, he had his hopes up.

Michael clicked on the message. It wasn't from

Linda. Instead, there was a picture of a beautiful young woman wearing nothing but a red bra and panties lying back on a bed, her face giving off a seductive smile. His insides tightened. Next to the picture was a message. HEY MICHAEL! I SAW YOUR PROFILE ON YAHOO PERSONALS AND THOUGHT YOU LOOKED SO!!!! HOT!!!! USUALLY I DON'T MAKE FIRST CONTACT BUT AFTER SEEING YOUR PROFILE I COULDN'T RESIST. HOPE YOU LIKE MY PICTURE. LET ME KNOW IF YOU WANNA START TALKING. HUGS AND KISSES! MICHELLE.

His fingers hovered over the keyboard for several seconds, unable to type. No girl had ever made first contact with him. That meant this time around would be different. She obviously wanted him and wouldn't stop talking one day. It was everything he had been hoping for when he had first put his picture up online. He had finally found someone.

* * *

Nancy Thurman was surprised by her son's joyful

attitude that morning. Lately Michael had seemed
depressed and spent most of his days locked in his
room. No amount of prying would get the reason
from him, but she had an idea that a girl was
involved. For a while she had considered
disconnecting his computer, which would force him
from the bedroom. Her husband, however, had
vetoed that idea. Michael was twenty two years old
and had bought the computer on his own. The time of
taking things away from their son was long gone and
they had to allow him to live his life his own way.
Nancy hadn't agreed but respected her husband
enough not to go about her plan. She had even kept
the questions to herself when one afternoon Michael
received a large box in the mail that bore a return
address of a strange, almost sexual sounding, costume
store.

Now, during breakfast, she had more questions, but
this time they were used to find out what had turned
Michael around.

"I got a message today from a girl that lives right
here in town. She saw my picture and profile online

and really wants to date me."

His excitement was obvious and this made Nancy happy. At the same time she had some reservations. She had never been comfortable with Internet dating. Something about it didn't sit well with her. It was better to meet people out in the real world, not through the computer.

"That's great," Nancy said. She hesitated. "Are you sure she's for real though?" That didn't sound right. "I mean, it isn't someone trying to hurt you is it?"

Frustration twisted around the excitement Nancy had been witnessing. "Mom," Michael said. "How many times do I tell you, it's not a bunch of freaks out there? The Internet is just a good way to break the ice. It's like going to a club and knowing everyone there is unattached and wants to meet someone."

Nancy had heard this explanation before but she still didn't like it. The Internet was just too filthy for someone to find happiness. If those girls couldn't find a guy in the real world then something wasn't right about them.

* * *

By nine, that night Michael still hadn't received a reply to the message he had sent back to Michelle and anxiety was beginning to set in. He told himself that the worry he felt was ridiculous because not everyone had access to the Internet twenty-four seven like him, but it didn't do much to calm his nerves.

Two hours passed and there still was no reply. Michael sat at his desk waiting, his instant messenger ready. The messenger would tell him when he had an email, and would also allow him and Michelle to talk with each other over the Internet.

Another hour passed without a message. During this time, Michael turned his chair so he could watch TV. His mind could never settle into anything though. Each second that passed was a second toward that wonderful sound that he was waiting for -- the strange musical note that would echo from his computer speakers when he got an email.

The sound never came.

Seconds turned to minutes, minutes to hours, until eventually, Michael couldn't take it any longer. He was too tired to stay up and wait for Michelle.

* * *

2 OFFLINE MESSAGES.

Michael stared at the computer screen. The message had arrived ten minutes after he had called it quits. If he had only stayed up and on he would have been able to talk with her.

He clicked on the first message.

MICHAEL, YOU THERE? HELLO, MICHAEL? OKAY, GUESS NOT. I'LL TRY AGAIN IN A LITTLE WHILE. MICHELLE.

Michelle's picture was next to the message. Michael stared at it for several seconds. If she were this beautiful on screen what would she look like in real life? He couldn't even begin to imagine.

....

The second message had arrived twenty minutes later.

WELL GUESS YOU'RE NOT COMING ON TONIGHT. I'M GLAD YOU LIKED MY PICTURE. CAN'T WAIT TO TALK WITH YOU AND . . . HEHE. WE SHOULD GET TOGETHER SOMETIME TOO. I'D LOVE TO MEET YOU. SEE YOU SOON, MICHELLE. PS. IF YOU LIKE THAT PICTURE I HAVE SOME OTHERS I THINK YOU'LL ENJOY.

Michael quickly typed a message. It read: *Sorry I wasn't on. I fell asleep too early. Are you always on at the same time? Let me know. By the way, we live so close we could easily meet. Do you like going to Borders? That's a good place to meet. I'll treat you to a latte if you like. Anyway, talk to you soon. Michael. PS: I would love to see the other pictures.*

* * *

"That's too bad," Nancy said while scooping some scrambled eggs onto Michael's plate. "You two should set up a certain time to talk, and let her know you don't like staying up late."

Michael shrugged. "I don't mind staying up late. If I'd known she'd be on at two thirty I would have waited."

"Two thirty?" Nancy hadn't realized he had stayed up that late. "What's she doing on the computer at two thirty?"

"I don't know. Some people don't go on until it's late." He started eating his eggs.

"Still, two thirty is pretty late. That's when all the predators are probably out." She took his glass and filled it with orange juice.

"Actually the scary people are on during the day because that's when they can talk with little kids. Being on late is safer."

Nancy didn't like the fact that Michael had this knowledge. She hoped it was just a theory and not something he knew for sure. "You want anything else?"

"No thanks."

* * *

1 OFFLINE MESSAGE.

Michael had tried so hard to stay up, but it had been no use. He had fallen asleep around ten twenty; a full two hours before Michelle had gone online.

I'D LOVE TO MEET AND I LOVE BORDERS. LET'S GO THERE TOMORROW IF YOU CAN. SOMETIME IN THE AFTERNOON OKAY? LET ME KNOW. SORRY THAT WE KEEP MISSING EACH OTHER. I NEVER KNOW WHEN I'LL BE ONLINE. SEE YOU TOMORROW, MICHELLE. PS: HERE'S THOSE PICS I PROMISED. ENJOY.

Michael clicked on the pictures and waited a minute while they downloaded. The first one came up. It was a picture of Michelle from the neck down. She wasn't wearing any clothing. Her body was beautiful. The second picture was one of her in a skirt and blouse, only the blouse was opened to reveal her breasts and the skirt lifted. It was more artsy than the first one and had a teasing quality that would grab any guy's attention.

There was a stirring in his testicles. Michael reached down and undid his pants. Five minutes later he stepped into the shower, a clean pair of underwear and pants waiting for him on his bed. While showering he wondered: *If I can get so turned on by pictures of her, what would happen once we are alone together?*

* * *

1 OFFLINE MESSAGE.

It was five thirty in the morning. Once again Michael had tried to stay up but failed. Once he had awakened that morning, however, he couldn't get back to sleep due to the excitement of meeting Michelle that afternoon.

The day before he had sent her a message that read: *Is two o'clock okay? I'll be waiting in the café area for you. By the way, I loved the pictures. Can't wait to see the real thing. The only thing that would have made them better would have been your face in them. You are so beautiful. Have any good ones with your face in them too? See you at two, Michael.*

MICHAEL. TWO O'CLOCK IS PERFECT. I'LL BE
THERE. I DO HAVE PICTURES WITH MY FACE
BUT NONE OF THEM ARE NAKED ONES. I DON'T
LIKE HAVING NAKED PICTURES WITH MY FACE
OUT THERE. HERE ARE A FEW 'SEXY' ONES
THOUGH. ENJOY. MICHELLE.

Michael looked at the pictures. They were Michelle
in different outfits, mostly underwear but some
fantasy costumes as well. Each one seemed sexier
than the previous and he actually liked them better
than the nudity ones she had sent. Something about
the hint of what was beneath the clothes was a big
turn on.

* * *

Nancy was excited for Michael, but also a little
nervous. Never before had he met someone from the
Internet and she hoped everything turned out okay.
Fear that this person was some strange demented old
man who wanted a twenty two year old boy as a
house pet wouldn't leave her system. She wished
Michael could have found girls in a more normal face-

to-face way.

Don't worry, everything will be okay.

Nancy took several deep breaths after thinking this and then went about cleaning the kitchen. While doing this she suddenly had a thought about Michael's new girlfriend (or whatever she was?). *What did she look like?*

She tried pushing the curiosity away, but couldn't, and started toward his bedroom.

* * *

Michael was too nervous to sit down. Instead he paced the café area of Borders, his eyes always drifting toward the entrance.

He had arrived ten minutes early for the meeting. That had been fifteen minutes ago. Now she was five minutes late. Each second that ticked by was horrifying. What if she didn't show?

Michael tried to concentrate on a magazine he had picked up from the Entertainment section. It had a feature column about the new *Harry Potter* movie, which had been out for a few weeks. Michael had gone and watched the movie with his mother. The two had enjoyed it. At the same time, he had been disappointed. He had hoped to see the movie with Linda. It would have been the first time he saw a movie with a girl other than his mother.

Maybe the next one will be with Michelle?

* * *

It had been a long time since Nancy had entered her son's room. Once he had turned eighteen her husband had told her that he needed his privacy and that she could not enter without permission. Now, she didn't care. She was too curious. And it was her house. She could go into any room she pleased.

A lot had changed over the years. Most of those changes had to do with the computer area.

Nancy didn't have a lot of experience with computers or electronics in general. In fact, she hadn't even been able to figure out how the digital camera

Michael had asked for during Christmas worked until he showed her that afternoon. Now she looked at that digital camera. He had set it up so it could take pictures on a timer. This concerned her. What kind of pictures was he taking that he didn't want her to see and needed a timer rather than a person to take?

She ignored this thought and went to his computer. A screensaver was illuminating the screen. She moved the mouse. The screensaver disappeared.

Nancy had never seen his desktop before. There wasn't much there. An icon link to the Internet was the first thing her eyes fell on. She double clicked it. Unfortunately, a password window came up and she couldn't figure it out.

Below the Internet icon was a small folder. The label said MISC. Nancy double clicked it. A screen with several folders appeared. Nancy read each one. Nothing jumped out at her. Randomly she began to click on them. Most were empty. She wondered why he had so many empty folders inside the MISC folder.

She clicked on a folder that brought her to a page

with more folders. This time the names made more sense. She scanned them. A folder jumped out at her. It was labeled MICHELLE PICTURES.

Nancy double clicked the folder. A second later, she screamed.

* * *

Michael felt tears running down his face as he stumbled toward his car. Deep down inside he had known this would happen. Something about him made it inevitable. No girl would ever agree to meet him. They all just liked to tease him to the point of extreme happiness and then let him go. It was cruel.

He started his car but didn't pull out right away. Nothing good was waiting for him at home. Nothing good was waiting for him anywhere.

In his mind, he pictured a car slamming into a brick wall at ninety miles an hour. The driver would never feel a thing, especially if he wasn't wearing a seatbelt.

The only thing that kept him from actually driving

into a brick wall at ninety miles an hour was the thought that maybe something had happened with Michelle. Perhaps she had wanted to come but her car hadn't started? After all, she had been the one to contact him. Maybe she wasn't just teasing him.

He decided to go home and find out.

* * *

"Just come home now," Nancy said into the phone after listening to her husband protest about leaving work early. "It's an emergency."

She hung up without waiting for a response. She had used Michael's phone. Her eyes drifted back to the computer screen. During her call, the screensaver had come back on. She hesitated. One touch of the keyboard and the MICHELLE PICTURES would be back. She didn't want to look at them again. She didn't want to see the pictures of Michael dressed as a girl ever again.

Sunburn

"Daddy, please! I don't want to do it." Tears fell from Jamie's eyes, the sight of which tugged at Donald's heart. "Please."

Donald shook his head and, in a voice that was as calm and soothing as he could manage, said, "I know honey, I know, but remember when you went to the doctor last summer and needed to get a shot. You didn't want to do that either, but you had to or else you would get sick and die. This is the same."

"But Daddy -- "

Donald cut her off by placing a gentle, yet firm

hand upon her mouth. "Shhh, honey, it's going to be okay. All right sweetheart? Listen to your Daddy, okay, I know what's best." With that, he removed his hand and replaced it with a homemade gag, which would allow both his hands to work as needed. He also covered her eyes with a strip of cloth, knowing treatments were always less traumatic when one could not see the actions taking place. "Okay honey, just take a deep breath and relax, it'll all be over soon, I promise."

* * *

Never before had Donald Weston experienced such an emotional mess. Less than a year earlier, after his wife died, he had assumed he never again would know such grief, yet now it had all returned; only it was ten times worse. It was one thing to watch his wife die, but completely another thing to watch his daughter take the same route. This time, however, he was not going to sit back and wait for the end, helplessly watching incompetent doctors fumble around with useless treatments. No. It was going to be different, for now he had taken matters into his own hands. The journey would still be a painful one, but this time the destination would not be death. Instead, it would be a long happy life full of everything a little girl could ever wish for.

* * *

Earlier that morning, fighting panic, Donald had set out to find the cure to his daughter's potential sickness. It came in the form of a woman named Debbie Starling, a thirty something woman who had no obvious signs of illness, and whose skin radiated with beauty. Two other possible cures had come in contact with him during his shift, but each had a flaw that Donald would not allow his daughter to receive. Unfortunately, he had realized, due to the short amount of time he had, he might have to settle for someone with flaws. The appearance of Debbie had put an end to that troubling thought.

* * *

Debbie Starling was having a bad day. It had all started before she woke up, when her thirteen-year-old son Steven had sneaked out of the house to hang out with friends. Of course, at one in the morning there wasn't much to do, so naturally their actions turned deviant. To make the situation worse, the group had decided against using water balloons on the passing cars in favor of eggs, which created a better *splat* in their opinions. It also created a harsher punishment when the police came since egg splatter could be considered vandalism.

Steven had been in tears when the police officer brought him home at three in the morning, but they did not calm the anger Debbie felt toward her son. Waking up at three in the morning was bad enough, but when it was the police pounding on the door it only got worse and worse.

Yet now that incident seemed so far away as her body slowly swayed in the upside down room, her head screaming in agony and throat raw from the eruptions of vomit, which was now piled beneath her on the cold concrete floor.

Fear tangled her mind. *What did the guy want from her?*

Though dizzy, she forced her chin toward her chest, which allowed her eyes to look up at her feet. The man had wrapped her ankles several times with rope while she had been unconscious and then had strung her up by them. At some point there had probably been pain due to the loss of circulation to her toes, but that had faded before she had awakened. Now it was as if her feet weren't there.

Handcuffs linked her wrists together behind her back. They weren't as tight as the rope around her ankles, yet were not loose enough for her to slip through them. Even if they were there would be no way for her to lift her body upward toward her ankles and free herself. Her cheerleading days were long gone, along with the flexibility and strength that had been required.

A smell other than vomit reached her nose. It was urine. A glistening sheen from it was present on her naked body. The stream had run down her stomach, and then went to the left of her dangling right breast where it then made it to her shoulder and dripped to the floor.

What does he want with me? she asked herself again.

The possibilities were endless.

Without warning, the door at the far end of the room opened and the man stepped in. He now wore a brown leather apron over some work clothes rather than the blue uniform she had first seen him in, and was carrying a strange bundle in his right hand.

Her eyes followed that bundle as he set it down on a small table that sat about three feet from her dangling body and unfolded it. A chill raced through her at the sight of what had been encased within.

"I'm sorry," the man said without turning, his eyes looking over the stainless steel contents of the bundle. "I would have gotten started while you were asleep, but had a question I needed to know first." He turned. "Now, please, answer truthfully. Have you ever had any type of suspicious growths removed from that beautiful skin of yours?"

Debbie was too frightened to speak.

"Debbie," the man said. "Please don't make me force an answer from you." He selected a thin blade from the bundle while saying this, which snagged her attention. "Now, have you ever had any suspicious growths removed from your skin, and if so, which area?"

Debbie shook her head, which caused the room to spin, and then said, "No." The word sounded terribly foreign; no doubt due to the position of her body and the rawness the vomiting had left.

"Very well," the man said. "Let's get started. Once again, I apologize that you have to be awake for this. If I was sure the operation would be a success I would kill you before getting started, but fear that I might need more skin in a few days and don't want to have to go find another woman like yourself. Now, this will only hurt for a second." With that, he moved the knife blade toward the skin of her left thigh.

* * *

Donald Weston had pulled two women over before getting the call to bring a young teenager home to his parents. The kid had been part of a group that was throwing eggs at cars and five officers had been needed to escort each individual.

Fearing that he would not find a woman in time that met his standards, Donald nearly ignored the radio call, but then realized that he would still need a steady job after Jamie's operation so that she could have a wonderful life. So, he had responded to the call and taken the kid home, and to his surprise met a woman who probably had the fairest skin of anyone he had ever seen. Making the situation even better was the fact that she didn't seem to have a husband (which was probably why her son was lacking so much discipline), so taking her later on would be simple.

The rest of his shift had gone by slowly. Around five he pulled over a young woman who also had wonderful skin and wrote down her address just in case the first woman, Debbie Starling, didn't work out. After that, he had patrolled the streets without a care until eight o'clock came around and his shift ended.

* * *

Not wanting to deal with her son after he was brought home by the police, Debbie had taken him to his father's house. Kevin had protested at the sudden drop off (out of earshot of Steven of course) but then reluctantly took him.

Debbie then went back home, her mind focused on having a quiet, relaxing Saturday. It was anything but relaxing.

Ten minutes after pulling into her driveway the cop who had brought Steven home returned. "I'm sorry to bother you ma'am, but I need you to come down to the station with me."

"What? Why?" Debbie asked.

"Well, the man whose car was hit wants to press charges and you and the other parents need to come down and talk with our captain."

Debbie's stomach sank. She couldn't believe it. Not only was she angry with her son, but now she was angry at the man who was pressing charges because egg splatter wasn't really that big a deal. "Okay, where is the station?" She had lived in Wheaton, Illinois almost her entire life, yet never had needed to know where the police station was prior to that morning.

"It would probably be easier for me to take you."

"Okay, whatever. Does my son need to come along?"

"No, just you. Is your son here?"

Debbie shook her head. "No, I dropped him off at his father's house earlier."

"Okay, great. Let's go."

* * *

Fearing the woman might vomit during the operation and then choke to death, Donald had made a gag out of a small rubber ring that he hoped would allow any vomit that came up to pass through the opening while at the same time keeping her screams from reaching the neighbors. It worked.

Afterward, he removed the homemade gag and went to where his daughter was strapped down to a table in the other room.

Jamie pleaded with him about the operation, but, like the woman in the other room, didn't really have a choice.

It was either this or go through the same terrible agony his wife had gone through as the skin cancer had slowly, and painfully, taken her life.

Donald bared the area of flesh that had been so badly burned the other day while Jamie had played with her friends, and doused it with alcohol. *Oh honey, why didn't you listen to me about the suntan lotion?* He asked silently while preparing to cut away the ruined flesh. *Especially after what your mother went through?*

His eyes drifted over to the skin he had taken from Debbie Starling and then to the spool of thread and needle he would use, his mind praying that the transplant would be a success. Then, without further hesitation, he lowered the scalpel to the edge of the sunburn on his daughter's leg and began the operation.

Red Pickup

"Don't worry Mom. I'll find a way. Just rest easy now."

* * *

"Why were you avoiding me?" Deputy Riley asked, his words turning to vapor in the cold morning air.

The boy looked at him. "Sir?"

"Back there on fifth. You turned to avoid me." He looked down at the boy's license. Stephen Fredric. Age eighteen, born August 16, 1983. Glasses. Organ donor. Everything seemed normal, but Riley had been a cop a long time and instinct was telling him differently. This boy had turned to avoid him, which meant he probably had something to hide. But what? It was this that made police work so dangerous; the

....

unknown.

"I just turned there. I'm on my way home."

Riley looked down at the registration card, glancing at the address. "You live on sixth, why'd you turn on fifth?"

"Back roads."

"Yeah . . . right."

"It's true." Saying *It's true* usually meant what had been said was a lie. The boy had been avoiding him.

"You been drinking tonight son? Is that it?" Riley wasn't going to let this kid go.

"No sir."

"Step out."

"I didn't do anything wrong." Now the boy was getting upset. This cop couldn't order him around like this, he had rights. Plus his mother, he had to hurry.

"Just step outside."

Stephen sighed and opened the door.

Riley watched the boy walk and decided he had not been drinking. But what did he have to hide? He looked the boy up and down and then looked at the truck. From where he was standing he could not see anything illegal inside and the truck bed was full of snow from last night's blizzard. He had nothing on this boy. But something was wrong.

"Any drugs inside?" Now he was just stalling, trying to figure this out.

"No sir."

"Those your cigarettes?" He pointed to the pack between the seats.

"I'm eighteen," the boy said.

"They yours?"

"My father's."

"Where is your father tonight? Is he home? I want to give him a call."

The boy shook his head. "He's not home."

"Where is he?"

"They went out."

"Where?"

"Dinner."

The last two answers were said quickly and Riley could see the boy was getting nervous. Why was that?

"Can I go now? I need to get home."

"What for?"

"I'm gonna be late."

"Late for what, son?" Riley asked again.

The boy looked at him for several seconds before saying, "A movie."

"I thought you were going home?" He had caught the boy in a lie now.

"I am. Movie's on TV."

"What movie?"

"Back to the Future." The boy looked at the ground as he spoke. Was he embarrassed, or did he not want to look him in the eye?"

"Have a seat in your car while I put this into the computer." Riley held up the license. He hadn't done this earlier because he had been sure the boy would give something away. Now he wanted more time to think.

The name came up clean. No warrants. Not even a speeding ticket. Maybe the boy was telling the truth.

If he was, then Riley felt bad. He had treated the boy like a criminal, but it had to be done. Expect everyone you pull over to have a gun in their glove box. His father hadn't. He had tried to treat everyone as if they were innocent and that was how he had gotten a bullet in his face.

What's under the snow?

The thought hadn't occurred to him before. All that

snow in there could hide something. Maybe that was
what the boy was worried about.

Riley got out of his squad car and began walking,
license and registration in hand, as if he was going to
give them back. He then veered to the right and
reached into the truck bed.

The boy hit the gas.

Riley jumped back while grabbing his gun.

The truck skidded at first, and then caught hold.

Riley ran back to his car. The chase had begun.

"Got one running on me, down fifth. Red truck.
Speeding over -- " he glanced at his own speedometer
" -- fifty miles on icy roads." He told the operator
everything, license number, the boy's age and name.
Everything, and that he was hiding something in the
truck bed under all the snow.

Up ahead the brake lights of the truck came on but
the truck was going too fast on the icy surface. Rather
than turning, the truck skidded off the road and into

the ditch, rolling as it did.

Riley's car skidded as well, but not as badly as the truck, which was overturned.

Cautiously, Riley exited the vehicle and walked around to the driver's side door. It was standing open. The boy was gone.

He looked to the right and left, trying to find tracks. About ten feet away he saw something sticking up out of the snow. It looked like a foot.

Five feet from that was an arm.

What the hell was going on?

Snow crunched behind him. Riley whirled around. He was struck across the face with something.

Nothing was right after that. First, there was blackness and then a bright light. Then pain.

When he awoke hours later, he was in a hospital bed.

A nurse walked in. "Oh, you're awake. Let me get

the doctor."

"Wait. Hold it a sec." His head screamed in agony. "What happened?"

"You were hit in the face."

"I know. What happened with the boy and the truck? All the bodies?"

"I better get the doctor."

"NO!" he screamed. "Tell me." For some reason he had to know.

"They didn't find the boy and I don't know anything about the bodies."

He wanted to ask how many there were, but wondered if he really wanted to know the number. Or worse, how long the boy had been driving around with them. With the weather they had been having, the snow could have been there for weeks.

The nurse left. A moment later, the doctor came in. The head wound was not bad, slight concussion. He would be back at work within a week.

Later that day Mike Walker, friend and co-worker, came to visit.

"The address checked out," Mike said while sitting on the edge of the bed.

"Yeah?"

"The boy wasn't there but we found his mother." Something in his eyes said this was going to be bad. They were right.

"She was dead."

Riley considered this for a moment then said, "The boy killed her?"

"Well, um . . . you could say that. You know those bodies that were in the back of the truck?"

He would never forget.

"They were from Oak Hill." Oak Hill was a cemetery on the edge of town. "After he hit you he dragged one of the bodies home and . . ."

Riley waited. Finally, he asked, "What?"

"The boy's mother needed a liver transplant. She'd been in and out of the hospital for some time by then but they couldn't do anything for her because there weren't any liver donors available."

Riley started to know where this was going.

"The boy tried it on his own." That was when Mike started to lose it. "God it was a mess. Her stomach had been cut open and blood was everywhere. In the wound the boy forced in the decaying liver of a dead woman." He took a deep breath. "The morgue guy says it looks like her heart failed after that and the boy tried CPR for a long time, all her ribs were broken."

Riley remembered the boy's urgency. He had been trying to get home quickly before his mother died. In the end it hadn't mattered.

"Did they find the boy?" Riley asked.

Mike shook his head. "It looks like he left after it didn't work."

"His father?"

Mike again shook his head no.

The Bone Yard

"Leo, stop!" Brian yelled from the couch. "I'm trying to watch this." On the TV screen a 'King of the Hill' episode was coming to an end. Brian loved the show and watched it every night at six thirty on channel eight.

Leo's whining continued, and grew louder with each passing second. Brian tried turning up the volume, but it didn't do any good. The sound from the TV was no match for the constant ear-piercing ring that echoed from the dog.

"It's not seven o'clock yet," Brian shouted.

It was no use, and a second later Brian turned off the TV and headed down into the entryway. Leo stopped his whining and looked up at Brian, a grin spreading across his long snout.

"You're a pain in the ass sometimes, you know that?" Brian said to the Sable and White Collie. "A real pain in the ass."

Leo didn't respond. He knew better than to believe a statement made in anger. Brian loved him, had loved him for the last three years. Nothing would ever change that.

Brian pulled out the leash from the closet and attached it to Leo's collar. "I know, I know," he said. "I'd be humiliated too, but it's the law." Three years earlier Brian wouldn't have followed the law that required dogs to be leashed, but lately the town's deputies had been stepping up the patrols and he was bound to cross their path several times during the evening stroll.

"Ready?" Brian asked.

Leo let out a *let's go* bark.

* * *

"Evening Mr. Tuttle," Deputy Parker said. The older deputy had pulled his car alongside Brian while Leo was lifting a leg to pee. "Out for your nightly exercise?"

"Yep." Brian didn't like talking to the police, even if it was just a small town cop. It was hard to judge their intentions, and he always worried that they knew more about him than they should. "A little exercise before bed, right Leo."

Leo didn't reply. His distrust for law enforcement ran even deeper than Brian's.

"Well, just make sure you clean up any, um, well solids." The deputy looked ahead while speaking and smiled when he saw a group of kids playing Kick the Can.

"Yes sir. Got a bag all ready for it." He pointed to his pocket where a small plastic grocery bag stuck out.

"Good. Well, have a nice evening." With that the
deputy headed on his way. Once out of earshot Leo
let out a mean growl. Brian agreed with Leo's distaste.

* * *

The neighborhood was full of children playing games;
only the games were not as widespread as they would
have been a few summer's earlier, and now parents sat
out on the front porches watching. Their concern,
however, didn't stop them from allowing their little
boys and girls to come over and pet Leo as the two
passed on the sidewalk. Leo pretended to enjoy the
attention.

Twenty minutes later, the two left the
neighborhood and entered the weedy scrubland that
connected several backyards to the forest that
surrounded the town. From that point on Leo was
leash free and ran several yards ahead of Brian,
anxious to get to the clearing in the woods. It didn't
take long.

"Hope no one stole it," Brian taunted while walking to the thorn bush where the small shovel was hidden. Leo let out a playful growl. For three years the thorn bush had kept the shovel hidden, and it would do so for many more.

Leo's excitement caused him to run around for a while before picking a spot, and then he began to dig.

Brian watched for several seconds and then said, "You want to dig it up, or should I?" It would take Leo a long time to dig down deep enough, but only seconds with the shovel.

Leo stepped aside and waited, his tail wagging.

Brian walked up to the small hole Leo had begun and stuck the shovel in. The dirt was loose and didn't take long to move. Once that was complete, Brian set the shovel aside and reached into the cold hole.

Leo spun in circles.

Brian pulled out the bone. Leo waited. Before tossing it he checked it over, his eyes searching for a clue as to where it had come from. The fact that it was part of a femur narrowed it down, but not to the point of identification; however, the small hatchet marks on the lower side did.

"Ah, I remember this one," Brian said. With that he threw the bone across the grassy clearing.

Leo gave chase.

The brown object flipped over and over for several seconds, loose dirt falling free, before crashing back down to the surface. Leo was on it instantly and ran it back to Brian.

"Ugh," Brian said as his hand pressed against a glob of sticky saliva. "You slobber too much."

The bone went flying.

Leo sprang after it.

Brian waited.

This time Leo didn't bring it back. Instead he sat on the grass and began chewing at an already worn area near the top. Brian wondered if there was a great deal of satisfaction in what Leo was doing. The bone, after all, had belonged to his previous owner, an abusive man who had struck the dog one too many times.

His mind replaced the clearing with an image from the past. In it Brian was driving home from his parent's home near Chicago when suddenly he heard someone calling for him from the town up ahead.

Without much thought he flicked on the turn signal and glided his car off the interstate and into the town of Fair Oaks. The house where the voice was calling from didn't take long to find, and soon Brian was at the front door, the hatchet from his trunk in hand.

Brian savored the bloody memory.

Leo returned with the bone.

"Jeez," Brian said while trying to find a dry spot on the slimly femur. There wasn't one and he had to settle for a less wet area. The throw was one of his best and nearly caused the bone to disappear into the trees.

Leo didn't give chase.

"What?" Brian asked.

Leo didn't say anything for several seconds. Once he did Brian took a step back while shaking his head. Leo knew what this meant and growled.

"I just got you a new one two weeks ago. What's wrong with it?" Most of the bones were difficult to find because they had been buried for a long time. However, the newest one was still fresh in his memory and he wouldn't need Leo's great sniffing skills to uncover it.

Leo let out a second growl.

"But that one *is* from a little girl," Brian said. In fact, the last three had been from little girls. What was Leo's fixation with little girls lately?

Silence engulfed the two.

Brian wanted to deny Leo's request but knew what would happen if he did. In fact, now that he thought about it, he figured Leo had probably chosen to play

with the bone of his former owner as a way of
reminding him what could happen if Brian displeased
him. This made him wonder if Leo's former owner
really had been abusive or if that was just a lie Leo had
told?

"Okay fine, but I can't do it until this weekend. The
boss is already breathing down my neck to get this
project done." Getting a new bone for Leo wasn't an
easy task. Not only did he have to hunt down
someone, kill them, and hack off the chosen limb; he
also had to set up a giant pot, boil the water, and
slowly work away the flesh, muscle, tissue, and
ligaments.

Leo seemed to understand and turned to get the
bone Brian had tossed. Once back, he dropped it in
the hole and then watched as it was reburied.

Before leaving the clearing, Brian took a look back.
The shadows had grown long since their arrival and
most of the clearing was dark. Even if it weren't dark,
Brian wouldn't have been able to pick out where all
the bones were buried.

Leo let out a soft bark. He wanted to get home so Brian could begin his plan for the next bone.

"How about Sara?" Brian asked later. Sara was a young girl that lived about two miles from their house. She loved dogs and would always come out to pet Leo if the two were walking by.

Leo liked this choice.

"Okay." Now all he needed was a plan. Leo would be part of it. That was the nice thing about having a dog that looked like Lassie. Kids couldn't resist coming over to him.

Once back in the neighborhood Brian attached Leo to his leash. Not long after that, the two were walking up the front steps of their home. Not a single kid had been out playing on the return trip. This wasn't unusual anymore. Once darkness was spotted, parents were quick to reel in their young ones. What else was to be expected in a town where children disappeared frequently?

Code Blue

Ronald Dempster was sitting on the toilet, holding his head in his hands, and grinding his teeth together when the alarm for a *Code Blue: Heart Failure* rang out beyond the room.

Footsteps echoed, along with some cart or stretcher being rolled down the hallway. Ron could hear everything as if it were in the room with him, which, of course, meant that the staff right outside the door had probably been able to hear the sounds he had been making a few seconds earlier.

The alarm continued to ring and masked the rush of water that echoed through the small bathroom as Ron flushed the toilet. Again, nothing but blood had come out during this midnight visit, though from the sounds one would have thought he filled the bowl.

Ron left the bathroom and walked toward the hospital bed his fiancé was sleeping in. Her body seemed at peace with the world, and had it not been for the IV and feeding tube lines one could easily think she was in her own bed in her apartment sleeping the night away.

This wasn't the case.

Kim Yearly, soon to be known as Kim Dempster, suffered from Cystic Fibrosis. Great strides had been made in the fight against the genetic disease. Once considered a childhood illness because people born with it wouldn't live past their first year, those with the illness now sometimes lived into their twenties or thirties, though a lot still lost the fight early on due to breathing complications.

Kim was twenty-two. She had done well thus far with a few mild setbacks, but because of the damage done to her lungs from repeated infections, she didn't have much longer to live and needed a new set of lungs. Her hospital visits were becoming much more frequent, and somewhat longer in duration.

"Hey," Kim said as Ron climbed back into bed with her. She was halfway asleep and wouldn't remember the conversation come morning. "You okay?"

"Yeah. Go back to sleep." He kissed her on the forehead and ran a hand through her hair.

She pulled his arm around her while forcing him to snuggle up against her and then drifted back to sleep. Normally guests weren't allowed to share beds with patients, but up on the Cystic Fibrosis floor exceptions were made.

Ron's statement had been a lie. He wasn't all right. Something was seriously wrong with him. The pain he had awoken to in his groin and lower stomach was intense, and the blood that had come out of him from both his penis and butt was frightening.

Grinding his teeth and praying that the Advil he had taken in the bathroom would kick in; Ron closed his eyes and tried to sleep. At the moment, it seemed an impossible task.

* * *

Two months earlier, it had been lower back pain with the occasional gut-wrenching stab into the groin. His doctor had assumed he had a kidney stone and told him he would have to wait it out. No kidney stone ever came out, however, and eventually the pain started to fade away.

Then a month later it came back, only this time it was more intense in the groin and lower stomach area. Rather than going to his crummy doctor, Ron had decided on seeing a specialist. Unfortunately, his insurance wouldn't cover the cost of seeing a specialist without a doctor's written approval, and when he went back to see his doctor no approval was written.

"You've just strained yourself," his doctor had said with a shake of the head. "Stay off it for a while and stop all the roughhousing with your friends."

Ron didn't roughhouse with friends, unless the bouncing around in the bedroom with Kim could be considered roughhousing, but it was impossible for him, at the age of twenty-two, to convince a fifty year old doctor of this, so he had just taken the advice and gone home.

Now, after seeing so much blood in the toilet so many times, he was going to demand that his doctor write him a referral because this was getting scary. As soon as Kim was done with her treatment, he was going to make an appointment.

* * *

Code Blue! Room 1130! Code Blue! Room 1130!

The words echoed through his mind as he opened his eyes, a terrible fog distorting everything within his head. Something was not right. Everything in the room was calm, yet behind his memory he could see chaos. Nurses were running about, a doctor was shouting orders, and someone else, a woman, was screaming. None of this was going on in the room, but for some reason he saw it clearly.

Room 1130.

They were in room 1130.

He shifted positions and looked over at Kim, only

she wasn't there. Blood marked an outline where she had been, along with a terrible substance that might have been fecal matter. Urine hung in the air.

"Kim!" he shouted while standing from the bed.

She wasn't in the room, nor was the IV pole, and the oxygen she usually took in through her nose at night had been shut off, the cord with its nosepiece dangling against the wall.

Oh God, Kim. Something awful had happened and for some reason he had slept through it, his mind only catching glimpses of things as it happened.

Ron ran out into the hallway, his voice shattering the two AM stillness as he demanded to know what had happened to Kim.

No one came to his aid.

He went to the nurse's station. Hillary, Stacy, and Mark were there, each one doing something different. Amid their work, the three were laughing about the ghost people sometimes claimed to see around the floor. Ron had heard about this wandering spirit

many times during his visits. Apparently, it was the

father of an eighteen-year-old Cystic Fibrosis patient

that was fading fast who had taken his own life in

hopes that his lungs would be right for a transplant.

"Hey, what happened to Kim?" Ron demanded.

The three went on laughing about the ghost.

"Hey!" he snapped. "What's going on here? What

happened to Kim?"

Again, there was no response.

Movement caught his attention. A man came out of

Kim's room. Ron raced over to him; questions about

Kim firing at random, yet the man, like the nurses, did

not say anything. He did, however, point down the

hall.

Ron went that way, though he wasn't sure why. If

something bad had happened, they would have taken

her to the emergency room. Down the hallway was

nothing but patient rooms.

The man stopped outside of the nutrition room, which also served as a break room for nurses. Most people didn't realize it, but the nurses didn't care if you went in to fill up a coffee mug or grab some tea or use the microwave or fridge, especially when you were a frequent visitor of a Cystic Fibrosis patient. Ron hadn't known this for a week and still cringed at the amount of money he had spent in the cafeteria below on coffee and snacks every day.

Crying and a separate voice of reassurance came through the closed door. Ron heard Kim. Frequent coughing pierced her sobs.

Ron entered the room.

Kim was sitting in the chair, her IV pole next to her, a portable breathing tank on the table delivering oxygen to her nose. A hospital consoler named Nancy that spoke with Kim often was consoling her.

"All the -- " coughing " -- blood -- " coughing " -- it was coming -- " coughing " -- everywhere -- " Kim couldn't finish due to a mouthful of mucus that came up and stuck in the back of her throat, and tried to force the glob from her mouth into a small cup she always carried.

"It's okay," Nancy said, her eyes trying not to concentrate on the mucus coming out. "He's going to be okay. They're working on him this very moment."

The man pulled Ron from the room. The two passed through the door rather than opening it, which, Ron hadn't noticed until then, was how he had been going through all the doors since waking up.

Fear tangled throughout his system. What was going on?

The man walked down the hall and took a right turn into the elevator area. Ron followed. They did not wait for an elevator. Instead, the man led him through the doorway to the stairs and down two floors to the emergency surgery level.

Chaos reigned.

His wasn't the only body being worked on. Illnesses and injuries didn't go by daytime work hours and kept the staff busy twenty-four hours a day, seven days a week.

Ron didn't care about the other patients, nor did he need the mystery man to lead him any longer and walked himself to his own body.

Doctors had his lower abdomen opened, his digestive organs exposed to all. Blood and fecal matter was everywhere. Had Ron the capability of throwing up he would have.

"Massive bowel blockage -- " someone started.

"Looks like scar tissue built up between the large and small until nothing could pass through," someone else said.

"What's his medical history?" someone else asked.

"Could be Crohn's Disease," someone suggested.

Amid the panicked shouting, there was a professionalism not many would be able to display in such a situation.

"They have control of everything," the man who had been leading Ron around suddenly said. His voice held no emotion, and spoke as if reciting something from a dictionary or encyclopedia.

"What?" Ron asked.

"Your body will go on living if you climb back in," the man said. "Or you can let it fade away and come with me back to the elevator and move on."

"Why wouldn't I want to live?" Ron asked, his mind a giant ball of confusion.

"Because it just so happens that your lungs would be a perfect fit for someone upstairs."

Startled, Ron stepped back. "What do you mean?"

The man didn't say anything.

"Are you saying she'll live if I walk away?"

The man shook his head. "That's not my call. Your lungs are healthy though, and I know they will be a match, but that's all I can say. I've already broken rules as it is."

Ron stood over his body and watched as doctors and surgeons went back and forth trying to repair him, knowing that their efforts would not be a success if he simply walked away.

His mind went back to Kim, the girl he loved, the girl he had asked to marry him. He had always said he would do anything to help her live longer, but the thought of sacrificing himself to save her wasn't an area his mind had explored.

He looked from his body to the man and then back to his body. A decision entered his mind. He didn't like it, but then again he wouldn't like either one.

* * *

Ron stood back as they lowered Kim's casket into the ground, the falling rain failing to land on his spiritual body. All her family was there, along with most of his and several friends of hers from the Cystic Fibrosis ward.

The seventeen-year-old girl named Gina that had gotten his lungs stood silently amongst the Cystic Fibrosis group. Five months had passed since her surgery and she was doing well.

Her father, the man who had led him around the hospital, stood behind her, his unnoticed hands on her shoulders. Ron had failed to recognize him that night even though he had seen pictures after the suicide.

"I'm not ashamed of what I did," the father said once the funeral was over. "You would have done the same if you could."

"You lied to me," Ron replied, five months of anger wanting to lash out.

"I didn't. I never said her name was Kim. Gina was ahead of her in every category on the list. You should have known that."

Ron shook his head and walked away.

Kim came up to him and took his hand. She had been with him ever since her body had given up the fight a week earlier.

Ron turned and looked into her eyes.

"You ready now?" he asked.

"Why wait," she said back.

He nodded.

Together they walked toward the light.

Wrong Turn

The girl seemed to appear out of nowhere around the blind turn and caused Glen to crash his bike into a mailbox, which, naturally, threw him head over heels into a prickly pine bush. The landing was not bad, but the needles that pierced and poisoned his skin with an irritating itchiness ruined his good fortune.

"What the hell are you doing?" Glen demanded while fighting his way from the bush. At three o'clock in the morning, one did not expect to find a young girl standing in the middle of the road. In fact, seeing a kid standing in the middle of the road, especially a blind turn like this, was always reason for concern.

The girl did not answer, nor did she look in his direction.

Free from the bush, Glen approached the girl. Had he still been a betting man, Glen would have put money on the girl being no more than ten. The t-shirt, overalls and red ribbon were a big clue, but also there was a strange familiarity surrounding the girl, which allowed him to know the age was actually nine. It was weird.

"You okay?" Glen asked, concern replacing his anger.

Again, the girl did not answer.

"Come on, let's get you out of -- " he reached for her while speaking and watched as his hand went through her flesh as if nothing were there.

The girl turned her head and looked at him with big bright eyes. "Glen, don't leave us again," she said.

Glen shouted while backing up, nearly tripping over his bike. A second later he was pedaling down

the calm Naperville streets, his adrenaline-laced fear
allowed him to reach speeds he had never before
achieved.

* * *

"You've got a week. If you don't have a job by then
you're out," Glen's father said the next night at
dinner.

"Robert," Glen's mother scolded.

"No," his father replied. "I'm sick of this. It's the
last time. He can't keep running back whenever he
has a problem."

Glen sat back and listened to the two bicker about
him. Normally he would be amused. This time
thoughts about the strange girl from the night before
and the fear that his father would make good on his
threat of kicking him out after a week disturbed him.

"It's not his fault they fired him," his mother said.
"Right, Glen?"

"Of course it isn't his fault," Robert snapped. "Nothing ever is. The 'F's on his report cards, the speeding tickets, the mean bosses, that night in jail -- nothing's ever his fault."

Getting fired had been his fault, but Glen wasn't about to admit it. He also wasn't sorry to see the job go. Washing dishes sucked. Now he just wished there was something else he could do so he could go back to living in his own apartment.

* * *

Thoughts of the girl got him riding again that night. Years earlier, when he had still been in grade school, Glen would sneak out of the house almost every night to ride his new bike. Now that he was back home, doing so again at night seemed important, almost as a way of capturing something he had long ago lost. It also helped take his mind off the fact that he couldn't keep a job to save his life.

The girl was waiting for him again. One moment the road was clear, the next she was there. This time

he did not crash his bike. Instead he skidded to a halt
and climbed down.

Her eyes followed him.

She was wearing the same outfit as the previous
night. It was the same outfit she had been wearing
years earlier when Glen had first met her, though the
circumstances of such a meeting were still beyond
him.

"What do you want?" Glen asked.

She didn't say anything.

"What do you -- " Glen stopped, his eyes focusing
on the house tucked into the trees behind the little
girl. Terror filled and chilled him to the core.

"Don't leave us again," the girl said.

* * *

Glen had tried college after high school, but failed
most of his classes. After that, he had started
working. Back then, his father had made the rule that

if he was in school he could still stay at home, but if
not he had to support himself like a real man.

Several years later he was back at home, living in
his old room, which his mother had left alone for some
reason, almost as if she had known he would fail in
the working world and need a place to stay.

This time around his father did not want that room
staying the same. He wanted it cleaned out. Anything
Glen didn't want could go into the garbage truck that
Friday.

That was why he was in his old closet the next
morning separating everything into two piles.
Halfway through the task he saw the girl again, the
image of her on the flimsy piece of cardboard. He
shouted, which drew his mother into the room.

"*Glen*, is everything okay?" she asked.

Glen scooted himself out of the closet, the HAVE
YOU SEEN ME postcard in his hands. Sweat was
dripping down his face, though most of that was from
the work he had been doing.

"Glen -- " she started again.

"I'm fine."

"What's that?" she asked.

Glen held up the postcard. "Do you know who she is?" he asked.

His mother examined the card. "It's from twelve years ago. It's -- " she stopped.

"What?" Glen asked.

"She's one of those kids that went missing that summer, back when you were, what, ten?"

Glen thought back. He had no recollection of a summer when kids had gone missing.

"Where did you get this?" she asked.

"It was in that box," he said while pointing into the closet. He then scooted back inside and pulled it out. Eight other postcards sat within, all of them showing a picture of a kid that went missing twelve years earlier from the Naperville area.

* * *

Glen waited until his parents went to sleep and then went for a bike ride again. As before, the girl was waiting for him.

The two did not speak. Instead, Glen stared at the house tucked into the dark trees. Terrible memories surfaced. He remembered himself kicking and screaming while a fat greasy man pulled him from the passenger seat of a car in the garage and into the house. He remembered being thrown into a bedroom with several other kids in it, all of them silent. He remembered the man coming for him later that day and taking him into another room where he eventually threw up because of the awful things the man did. He then remembered realizing the door to that room hadn't latched and sneaking out while the man was getting some paper towels to clean up the vomit.

Tears fell from Glen's eyes as he stared at the house. He had left all the other kids to fend for themselves and never told a soul. Several times he had ridden his bike back to the house with his father's gun, ready to go in and rescue everyone, but each time he had chickened out. On TV and in the movies kids could be brave, but in real life they were often cowards.

Glen looked back at the girl.

"I'm sorry," he said.

She looked at him.

"I was only ten," he said. "I was scared."

She continued staring at him.

"What? I can't change the past."

She pointed at the house. "Don't leave us, Glen."

Glen looked at the house. A light was on in one of the windows. It hadn't been earlier. Someone was still inside.

* * *

A high-pitched scream echoed from within the house as Glen approached the front door. Several more screams followed, all of them from what sounded like a grown man.

Glen tried the door. It was locked.

He looked back. The road was difficult to see from the front door because of the bushes and trees, though the girl's sudden brightness seemed to shine through all of it.

The screaming faded.

"I'm gonna rip your head off you little bastard!"

It was the fat man. Glen had heard his voice twelve years earlier and even though his mind had blocked everything for so long, there was something about the voice that he would never forget.

"You hear me!"

Glen kicked the door.

It didn't bust open like he had seen so often in the movies. Two more kicks loosened the hinges and caused some splintering. Two more broke a hinge, and another broke the door from the frame.

The house went silent.

Glen headed inside.

Almost instantly, he came upon the fat man who was standing in the hallway. One hand covered his right eye, blood and puss dripping down; the other held a wicked looking Buck knife.

"What the fuck!" the man said. He raised the knife.

Glen wished he had brought his father's gun.

Enraged, both from the pain and Glen's sudden intrusion, the man charged.

Sheer luck caused Glen to twist out of the way at the last second and avoid being sliced by the razor edge. He then tackled the man from behind, his courage rising up from nowhere.

The man shouted while falling to the ground, his fat body cushioning the fall. A little more fat and the man might not have been wounded so badly by his own knife, but some recent dieting worked against him.

Impaled, the man squirmed on the ground. He then managed to roll over and pull the knife from his body. Blood gushed. An acidic smell struck. His stomach had been punctured.

Glen looked up at the man's face. One of his eyes was missing. Despite this, Glen could tell it was the same man from his past, the same one who had ruined his life all those years ago.

He couldn't help himself. He kicked the man as hard as he could, first in the balls and then in the face. He continued kicking him until all movement ceased.

Exhaustion hit.

The surge of adrenalin faded.

Glen started to leave the house, but then stopped and walked back in. The door to the bedroom was closed. He stared at it for several seconds before twisting the knob.

The lock popped.

The door opened.

Panicked, a young boy of about eleven stood in the corner of the room, a small pocketknife in his hands. The blade was tiny, but had been enough to pierce the eye of the fat man.

"It's okay, I'm not going to hurt you," Glen said.

The boy didn't say anything.

Glen came forward and reached out a hand to the boy. The boy sliced at it with the knife. "Don't touch me!"

Glen backed up, hands in the air. He realized he didn't have to escort the kid out. The fat man was dead and all the doors between the kid and the street were either broken down or unlocked. Nothing would prevent him from escaping.

Outside the girl was gone.

Glen wondered if she had truly ever been there.

Afterward

There we have it my friends, ten dark tales that hopefully brought about a momentary escape from reality and produced a fear response within the brain that was enjoyed. And now, for those that are interested in the story behind the story, I shall share the background of each piece - as best as I can recall them.

Redstone Lake: this particular tale was written in late 2004 / early 2005 and has been one of my most rejected pieces given that most editors felt the subject matter was too explicit for their publications. Eventually, however, persistence paid off, and in 2009 an editor with Ghostlight Quarterly decided to use it in their premier issue.

Rest Stop: this quick tale, which earns quite a bit of 'what happens next' inquiries from readers, was the result of needing a short piece of fiction for a creative writing class that I was taking in college during the spring of 2006. I began writing it at five in the morning, and finished it by eight. The class began at nine. My fondest memory of this tale comes from reading it to the class, and then casually mentioning that I had written it that morning. Hearing this, a fellow student threw up his arms in frustration and loudly said that he would spend weeks trying to write two to three pages of interesting prose while here I had churned out a complete and exciting tale within three hours. With that, he walked out of class, door slamming behind him, leaving me stunned. Now, if only it truly were that easy. Writing a story that quickly was a rarity brought on by desperation. Two years later, the story was supposed to appear in an anthology about horror in Midwest, only the publication never got off the ground following the acceptance.

Jacob's Gift: my second published tale, one that I wrote during my senior year in high school. To this day, I have no idea where this story came from. At the time, I had an independent study in creative writing, and this story popped out one week while I was blocked with a novel titled *Forgotten Ritual*. In 2004, the story was published by Black Petals Magazine.

The Phone Call: toward the end of 2005, I met up with a fellow college student who I was friends with named Jen for lunch. We hadn't seen each other in several months given our new class schedules and her Cystic Fibrosis, which often required long hospital stays. During that lunch, I told her about my own illness, which she hadn't know about and then out of nowhere asked if she would like to go out on a date with me. She said yes. Given how sick we both were, that date saw us going to her apartment and watching *Pirates of Caribbean.* The next day, I left her a message letting her know I had had a great time and asked if she would like to get together that night as well. After that, the phone was silent for about eight hours, my eyes staring at it, willing it to ring, fear that it wouldn't flowing through me. This story was written by hand while waiting for that call.

The Other Side: this story was born out of my 2004 / 2005 frustrations with the new world of online dating. Every girl who seemed interested in me would always vanish, often after agreeing to meet up with me for lunch. I have no idea how many 'no show' moments occurred, but there were enough to form the inspiration for this story, which was written in the spring of 2005. Following that, as was often the case in 2005 and 2006, the story was accepted, but never saw publication due to the magazine folding before the story was to be published. Interesting side note: though I didn't realize it until just now, those frustrations with the online dating world also formed the basis for my 2012 novel *Nikki's Secret*, which, of course, explored a much darker theme on what could happen should one be teased to the point of madness by the false promise of a future relationship.

Sunburn: as mentioned in my introduction, the pain I was suffering from in 2005 led to me writing several stories that were very dark and horrific. This was one of them, and, in my opinion, the best of that era. It also earned me a nasty rejection letter given that I accidently gave the main character the same name as a famous author that I had been unknown to me at the time (Donald Westlake . . . now I love his work). Following that, the editor at that particular magazine refused to read anything I submitted, a letter actually telling me that he had no interest in ever reading or publishing anything by me and to stop sending him stuff. *Ouch!*

Red Pickup: my first ever published story. The inspiration for this tale came while walking in the high school parking lot after a blizzard. A truck in that parking lot had a bed full of snow, and, upon seeing that, I said to my brother, "How many dead bodies do you think could be hidden beneath that snow?" "I have no idea," he replied, but I'm sure you'll write a story answering that soon. He was right. I wrote that story, submitted it, and after two years of writing and receiving nothing by rejection letters from magazines, received my first acceptance letter. I was eighteen years old. A year later, Black Petals Magazine published the story.

The Bone Yard: in 2005, during a creative writing class, a fellow student wrote a story about an old man enjoying a walk with his dog. Upon finishing it, he turned to me and said, "Even you couldn't turn such a pleasant walk with a dog into a nightmare." I thought differently, asked his permission to give it a go, and, upon publication of the story in 2006, gave him a copy of the magazine, which he enjoyed.

Code Blue: one of my most personal stories, this tale originated in January of 2006 during a sleepless night in a hospital room where I was staying with my girlfriend Jen who was undergoing a two-week treatment for her Cystic Fibrosis. My inability to sleep was due to the pain my own disease was causing, and, rather than keep Jen awake while tossing and turning in her tiny hospital bed -- that's right, we just slept together in the same hospital bed, rules be damned -- I sat in the chair and wrote. A year later, in late 2007, the story was published by Zen Films in their *Love & Sacrifice* anthology. Jen and I were married by this time, awaiting her double lung transplant, which she received on January 17, 2008. In 2009 she died from rejection.

Wrong Turn: one of the oldest stories in this collection, "Wrong Turn" began during my senior year in high school after I saw some Missing Persons postcards in the mail. Given the subject nature, no one ever wanted to publish this tale, though many editors did praise it. A few even suggested I lengthen it into a short novel. In the end, I decided not to turn it into a novel and, knowing it was good, simply waited until I could include it in a collection one day.